Thank you to the generous team who gave their time and talents to make this book possible:

Author
Jewel La Porte and Theresa La Porte

Illustrator
Laurena La Porte

Creative Directors
Caroline Kurtz, Jane Kurtz, and Kenny Rasmussen

Translator
Alem Eshetu Beyene

Designer
Beth Crow

Ready Set Go Books, an Open Hearts Big Dreams Project

Special thanks to Ethiopia Reads donors and staff for believing in this project and helping get it started-- and for arranging printing, distribution, and training in Ethiopia.

ISBN: 978-1705977422
Library of Congress Control Number: 2020917955

Republished: 10/10/20

Big Plans

ትላልቅ እቅዶች

English and Amharic

"Little Brother, Uncle gave me an egg. I have a good idea," said Sister.

"ትንሹ ወንድሜ! አጎታችን እንቁላል ሰጥቶኛል። አንድ ጥሩ ሀሳብ አለኝ" አለች እህትዬው።

"Would you like to have our own little chicks?" she asked.

"የራሳችን የሆኑ ትናንሽ ጫጩቶች እንዲኖሩን ትፈልጋለህ?" ስትል ጠየቀች።

"Oh yes!" said Brother. "Then we could play with them. Where would we get our own chicks?"

"እንዴ አዎ!" አለ ወንድምዬው። "ከእነርሱ ጋር ልንጫወት እንችላለን። ጫጩቶቻችንን ከየት ማግኘት እንችላለን?"

"Well, where do chicks come from?" Sister asked.

"መልካም! ጫጩቶች የሚገኙት ከየት ነው?" ስትል እህትዬው ጠየቀች።

"ከእንቁላል ውስጥ ነው የሚፈለፈሉት?" አለ።

"Yes," she said. "The chickens sit on the eggs. We could take turns sitting on this egg."

"አዎ" አለች። "ዶሮዎች እንቁላሎችን ይታቀፋሉ። እኛም ተራ በተራ ይህንን እንቁላል መታቀፍ እንችላለን።"

"In a few days, we will have our own little chick. We can hatch more eggs later."

"በጥቂት ቀናት ውስጥ የራሳችን የሆነ ትንሽዬ ጫጩት ይኖረናል። በቀጣዮም ብዙ እንቁላሎች እንዲፈለፈሉ ማድረግ እንችላለን።"

Little Brother smiled.
"I want twelve chicks."

ትንሹ ወንድሜ ፈገግ አለ።
"አሥራ ሁለት ጫጩቶች እፈልጋለሁ።"

The children found a basket.
They put the egg in the basket.

ልጆቹ ቅርጫት አገኙ፡፡ በቅርጫቱ
ውስጥ እንቁላሉን አስቀመጡ፡፡

Then Sister carefully
sat on the basket.

ቀጥሎ እህትዬው በጥንቃቄ ቅርጫቱ
ላይ ወጥታ እንቁላሉን ታቀፈች፡፡

"Goodbye,"
Brother called.
"I'm going to play."

"በይ ደህና ሁኚ!"
ሲል ተጣራ
ወንድምዬው:: "ወደ
ጨዋታ መሄዴ ነው::"

"Okay, but come back soon!" Sister said.

"እሺ፤ ግን በቶሎ ተመለስ!" አለች እህትዬው።

She sat for a long, long time.
"It's your turn," she called.

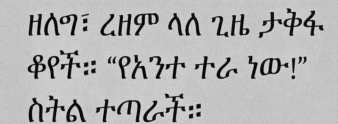

ዘለግ፤ ረዘም ላለ ጊዜ ታቅፋ
ቆየች። "የአንተ ተራ ነው!"
ስትል ተጣራች።

But Brother wanted to play.
"Wait," she said. "Think of the baby
chick we will have." So he sat.

ወንድምዬው ግን መጫወት
ፈልጓል። "ቆይ" አለች።
"የሚኖሩንን ትናንሽ
ጫጩቶች አስብ እንጂ"
ስለዚህም እንቁላሉን ታቀፈ።

Then Sister sat.
Then Brother
sat again.

ከዚያ ቀጥሎ ደግሞ እህትዬው ታቀፈች።
እንደገና ደግሞ ወንድምዬው ታቀፈ።

After a long time, Mama called them to eat.

ከረጅም ጊዜ በኋላ እማማ ምግብ ይበሉ ዘንድ ጠራቻቸው።

"I want to go eat," Brother said.

"ሄጄ መብላት እፈልጋለሁ" አለ ወንድምዬው።

"I want to go eat, too,"
Sister said.

"እኔም ሄጄ መብላት እፈልጋለሁ"
አለች እህትዬው፨

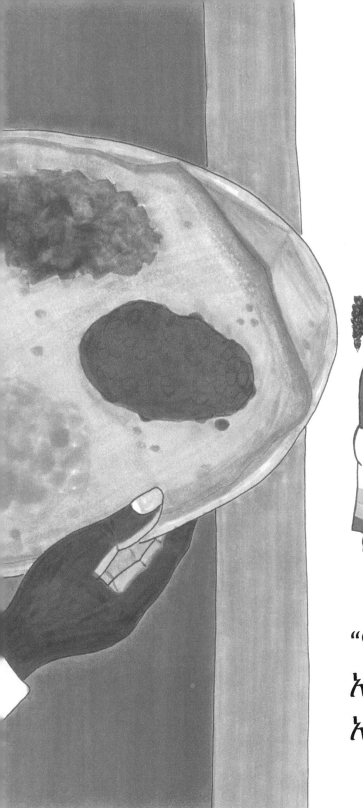

"No, you stay. I'll go eat," they both said at the same time.

"የለም! አንተ ቆይ፡፡" ፤"የለም! አንቺ ቆይ፡፡" ፤ "እኔ ሄጄ እበላለሁ" አሉ ሁለቱም በአንድ ላይ፡፡

"Come children," Mama said. "The egg will be fine while you eat."

"ልጆች ኑ" አለች እማማ። "በምትመገቡበት ጊዜ እንቁላሉ ምንም አይሆንም።"

After dinner, they were both too sleepy to sit on the egg.

ከራት በኋላ ሁለቱም እንቅልፍ ተጫጭኖቻው ስለነበር እንቁላሉን ለመታቀፍ አልቻሉም።

Sister said, "The egg will be fine while we sleep."

"በምንተኛበት ጊዜ እንቁላሉ ምንም አይሆንም።" አለች አህትዬው።

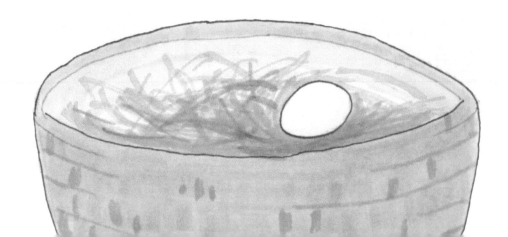

The next few days were too busy for egg sitting.

በቀጣዮቹ ጥቂት ቀናት እረፍት አጡና
እንቁላሉን ለመታቀፍ አልቻሉም፡፡

The egg never did hatch.

እንቁላሉ በጭራሽ አልተፈለፈለም።

"That is okay," Sister said, "Twelve chicks would have been a lot of work."

"ምንም አይደል" አለች እህትዬው። "አሥራ ሁለት ጫጩቶች ብዙ ሥራ ሊያስከትሉ ይችሉ ነበር።"

About The Story

Many creative children all over the world have tried hatching eggs. This book is based on author Jewel LaPorte's own childhood experience and the similar childhood experiences of her friend, Dora Dawson.

Because 7-year-old Jewel's uncle was a farmer, Jewel knew that eggs take many days to hatch. She didn't know that eggs must be frequently rolled or kept warmer than human temperatures (98 degrees). Since the hen's body is between 105-106 degrees F, the eggs are between 100-101 F when they are tucked under her. The hen also turns and adjusts the eggs many times a day so they will be evenly warm. Rolling also keeps the embryos in the nutritious egg whites, and it prevents them from sticking to the membranes.

Little Jewel was right that hatching eggs is a lot of work. Brooding hens usually sit on their eggs day and night for 21 days and only leave to eat, mostly at dawn and dusk.

To find out more about this process, visit:
- https://extension.psu.edu/how-the-chicken-incubates-eggs-naturally
- https://www.fresheggsdaily.com/2016/04/how-often-should-i-turn-my-hatching-eggs.html

About The Authors/Illustrators

This book is for Amelie, our Ethiopian-born granddaughter and niece.

Jewel LaPorte is a retired grade-school teacher, with a specialty in dyslexia. One of the things she enjoyed most was teaching kids how to read because reading holds the key to success in school. Little Jewel's egg hatching attempts have amused all of her grandkids, even though none of the eggs ever hatched.

Theresa LaPorte remembers the excitement and challenge of learning to read. She hopes to encourage and support new readers through her involvement in RSG books.

Laurena LaPorte hopes to share her love of books and art with kids through this RSG Books project. She cherishes her role as auntie to 11 nieces and nephews.

About Open Hearts Big Dreams

Open Hearts Big Dreams began as a volunteer organization, led by Ellenore Angelidis in Seattle, Washington, to provide sustainable funding and strategic support to Ethiopia Reads, collaborating with Jane Kurtz. OHBD has now grown to be its own nonprofit organization supporting literacy, innovation, and leadership for young people in Ethiopia.

Ellenore Angelidis comes from a family of teachers who believe education is a human right, and opportunity should not depend on your birthplace. And as the adoptive mother of a little girl who was born in Ethiopia and learned to read in the U.S., as well as an aspiring author, she finds the chance to positively impact literacy hugely compelling!

About Ready Set Go Books

Reading has the power to change lives, but many children and adults in Ethiopia cannot read. One reason is that Ethiopia doesn't have enough books in local languages to give people a chance to practice reading. Ready Set Go books wants to close that gap and open a world of ideas and possibilities for kids and their communities.

When you buy a Ready Set Go book, you provide critical funding to create and distribute more books.

Learn more at: http://openheartsbigdreams.org/book-project/

Ready Set Go 10 Books

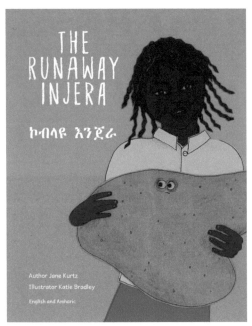

In 2018, Ready Set Go Books decided to experiment by trying a few new books in larger sizes.

Sometimes it was the art that needed a little more room to really shine. Sometimes the story or nonfiction text was a bit more complicated than the short and simple text used in most of our current early reader books.

We called these our "Ready Set Go 10" books as a way to show these ones are bigger and also sometimes have more words on the page. The response has been great so now our Ready Set Go 10 books are a significant number of our titles. We are happy to hear feedback on these new books and on all our books.

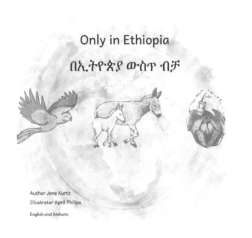

About the Language

Amharic is a Semetic language -- in fact, the world's second-most widely spoken Semetic language, after Arabic. Starting in the 12th century, it became the Ethiopian language that was used in official transactions and schools and became widely spoken all over Ethiopia. It's written with its own characters, over 260 of them. Eritrea and Ethiopia share this alphabet, and they are the only countries in Africa to develop a writing system centuries ago that is still in use today!

About the Translation

Alem Eshetu Beyene taught translation at Addis Ababa University for three years and translated six books during that time. He also has taught Amharic and written a book titled Amharic For Foreign Beginners. In addition, he has published a number of books for children that can be found in bookshops in Addis Ababa (and two on Amazon.com) and in schools where he donates copies for families that cannot afford to buy them.

Find more Ready Set Go Books on Amazon.com

To view all available titles, search "Ready Set Go Ethiopia" or scan QR code

 Chaos

 Talk Talk Turtle

 The Glory of Gondar

 We Can Stop the Lion

 Not Ready!

 Fifty Lemons

 Count For Me

 Too Brave

 Tell Me What You Hear

CPSIA information can be obtained
at www.ICGtesting.com
Printed in the USA
LVHW071813271020
669963LV00002B/79